Disclaimer

This is a work of fiction. Names, characters, organizations, spots, occasions and occurrences are either the results of the creator's creative energy or utilized as a part of an invented way. Any similarity to real people, living or dead, or genuine occasions is absolutely adventitious.

ISBN:
eBook: 978-1-946792-24-2
print:978-1-946792-25-9
audio/d :978-1-946792-26-6

Table of Content

SINKING ROSES

CHAPTER 1

Andrew, a 26 year old entrepreneur/investor, flew to his sister's house a day earlier to attend the California Governor's soiree. He attended the function with Tasha, his 24 year old sister.

While enjoying themselves at the soiree, Tasha met Nick – her ex-boyfriend from college. She introduced him to Andrew as an old pal. Nick was with Viola – his fiancé and colleague at the bank.

Meanwhile, Andrew had taken particular notice of Viola, dressed in a gorgeous cream colored dinner wear. Nick asked for a moment with Tasha to discuss some matters from the past. Andrew capitalized on that opportunity to chat Viola.

They exchanged contacts and found themselves a seat under one of the beautiful trees when Tasha and Nick were nowhere to be found. After about an hour, Andrew and Tasha located them. They went their separate ways and reintegrated into the crowd.

Having arrived home after the function, Andrew just couldn't get himself to stop thinking over Viola. Although she had told him Nick was her fiancé, that didn't stop him from feeling amorous towards her. The next morning, after having yearned throughout the night to speak with her, he picked up his phone and called her.

But to his disappointment, though she answered and spoke with him, she was hasty; not particularly interested; and told him she's got a busy day and couldn't afford to waste time on phone. The story remained pretty much the same, throughout the week, until the weekend. She agreed to meet him 2pm on Saturday at a restaurant.

Andrew arrived at the restaurant thirty minutes earlier than 2pm on Saturday, but she was over thirty minutes late. She joined him at the table and a waitress attended to them. They made their orders and dined together, smiling and chatting happily throughout. Viola, so passionate about her profession, was virtually speaking about her work the whole period. After having heard about just enough of her work-life, Andrew asked to know more about her personal and social life. She told him she didn't have a really rosy social life; very few friends and no close friend at all except Nick who doubled as her fiancé.

Andrew began to talk about his personal life though she never asked but while he did, it was obvious she wasn't interested. Moments later, Nick called her via her cellphone.

She picked up the call and they chatted excitedly for about ten minutes, leaving Andrew all by himself with a silly look on his face. After ending the call, she told him she had to leave to meet up with her fiancé.

Andrew was so jealous and a bit disappointed. He accompanied her to her vehicle and requested of her if they could meet the following day but her answer was in the negative. She told him she was gonna spend the weekdays with her fiancé and wouldn't have time for anyone else. She hugged Andrew, thanked him, and then set off in her car.

Andrew drove back to the house but upon reaching, it seemed as though there was no one home but earlier, Tasha had not spoken of going out. He knocked on her door but there was no answer. Then, he searched the other parts of the house but she was nowhere to be found.

He called her cellphone but there was no answer. He walked back to her room, opened the door and as he neared the bathroom to check if she was in there, she began calling his phone.

He answered and she told him something came up and she had to go check up on someone but then she was already on her way home. While walking out, a few books and magazines on her bed caught his attention. He sat on her bed, took them and began to flip through.

A picture fell from one of the books and he picked it up. It was an old picture; which showed Tasha and Nick in a romantic pose. There was an inscription behind: *"The love of my life. Nothing will ever break us apart. Tasha & Nick."* He wondered when but it looked like during Tasha's college years. The doorbell rang, he placed the picture back into the book and walked out to go check on who was at the door.

He opened the door and it was Evelyn, a friend of Tasha's which he had spoken to at the soiree. Although surprised to see him there, she smiled excitedly upon seeing him. He smiled back and let her in. She sat on a cushion chair at the hall while he put on the TV and when he was done, he took a seat in the chair next to hers and they began to chat.

'Andrew, I thought you wouldn't be here by now. Weren't you scheduled to leave the day after the party?'

'Yea, exactly, but something came up and I had a change of mind.'

'Okay, that must be something interesting. I hope I'm not being too nosy?'

'Umm... maybe you are, but it's not necessarily a crime. Is it?'

'Anyway, how have you been? I came to see Tasha; she around?'

'Oh I've been just fine. Tasha isn't home presently but she said she was gonna be back soon.'

'Okay, that's nice. I guess you'd have to keep me company until then.'

'Yea, I guess so.'

They chatted and chatted, so excitedly that they didn't even realize the clock tick. Around 7:30pm, after they'd called her again and had confirmed she was gonna come, Andrew went to fetch some grilled chicken and fruit juice from the kitchen. They dined together in the cushion chair.

The TV station put the *TITANIC* movie on the screens, Evelyn hopped out of her chair to join Andrew in his and they watched it together.

It was a serene and romantic mood in the hall, stemming from the movie they were watching and as it progressed, Evelyn could not stop herself from shedding tears.

He cuddled her in his arms and just some few minutes after the movie was done, she dozed off.

CHAPTER 2

Evelyn woke up in the middle of the night and found herself in the guests' bedroom. She checked her watch and the time was 1am. She wondered how and when she got there. She got out of bed to go check if Tasha had returned. As she made her way through the hallway to Tasha's bedroom, she heard the sound of the TV and could tell there was someone at the hall. She walked into the hall and met Andrew still sitting in the cushion chair and watching TV.

'Hey' she said.

'Hey, you're awake already?'

'Yea, you've not slept yet?'

'No, just watching this last movie before I do.'

'Okay, did Tasha return yet?'

'Umm… She hasn't and she is not answering her phone.'

'Oh, really? That's bad. Are you worried?'

'Quite worried… Just a little.'

'Oh, she's gonna be alright. She's a big girl and she's been living on her own for some time now.'

'Okay, I pray so.'

'Certainly. I think I have to go take a shower. I feel uncomfortably sweaty. I'll join you later.'

'Alright, it's okay by me.'

She returned to the bedroom, stripped off her clothing, and went into the bathroom. She put on the shower but there was no water. She tried and tried and tried but it just wouldn't work. She got out of the bathroom, wrapped herself in a towel, and made her way to the hall.

'Hey' She said while approaching him, 'can you help me with the shower? It's not working.'

Andrew turned about to look at her; he saw her wrapped in a white towel which covered the top of her breasts to just beneath her butts. He was flabbergasted by her sexy tantalizing body. She caught him drooling lustfully at her thighs but ignored it.

She took the lead while he followed and all the way through, he just couldn't get his eyes off her buttocks and thighs.

Upon arriving, he checked the shower but couldn't locate where the problem was. He told her he couldn't get his way around it but she was worried; she really had to take a shower. Andrew suggested she may have to do that in his bathroom. She agreed to it and he led her into his bedroom. He checked his shower – everything worked fine – showed her into the bathroom and walked out of the room, leaving the door to the room ajar.

After about fifteen minutes, she walked out of the bathroom and made her way to the hall.

She stood behind him, leaning on the chair in which he sat, and then asked 'Hey, do you like what you saw?'

'Pardon?' He said, turning over his shoulders to look at her.

'Do you feel satisfied after seeing me naked?'

'What do you mean? Did I...?' He said innocently.

'Huh... Really? You thought I wouldn't see you? You returned to the room and with the door to the bathroom partly opened, you peeped. Your shadow was very visible. I just decided to ignore you. It's not, at the least, honorable thing to do.'

He covered his mouth with his hands, in shock and shame, and said 'Oh my God! Look, I'm so sorry. I feel so ashamed.'

'Exactly, I think you should be. Anyway, I'll need a little help with something.'

'What is it?' He said, unable to look her in the face.

'I need to apply some lotion to my skin but I think there's none in the guests' room.'

'Oh. I will get you mine.'

'Ha-ha, no please, no. Tasha and I use the same kind of lotion. When I sleep over or she at my place, we share the same lotion. I prefer getting hers.'

'Okay, so you're suggesting I take you to her room?'

'Exactly. She'll have no problem with that.'

Andrew's dick was already hard erect because of Evelyn's partially naked sexy body standing right before him. He stood up quickly and took the lead, hiding his erection from her, and walked her to Tasha's bedroom.

She made her choice from the various lotions and cream in Tasha's drawer, sat on Tasha's bed and asked Andrew to apply the lotion to her skin. He was reluctant but she insisted.

He applied the lotion to her arms and chest and then bent down to apply them on her legs. He squatted to apply on her feet and legs but as he did, he caught a view of her freshened neatly shaved vagina staring back at him just beneath her towel – His dick hardened the more. He smeared her legs, still stealing glimpses at her beautifully shaped pussy, and made his way towards her knees.

After smearing on her knees and lower thighs, he said 'I think you should take it from here.'

'Why do you think so?

'Because… It's more private around there.'

'You don't want to see my nakedness? What is there to hide if you've already seen them? Just go on with it, okay.'

'Come on, no. I'm sorry for what happened back there okay?'

Ignoring to reply him, she turned around, laid upon her belly on the bed and signaled to him to smear the lotion on her. He waited a few seconds, pondering what to do next, and then sat by her on the bed. The towel laid midway on her butts; everything was visible and he could see her vagina lips sandwiched between her butts. He smeared the lotion on her thighs, shifted the towel completely off her butts and smeared her butts too. Then he stopped and asked, 'Do you realize for a moment that you are seducing me?'

She stuck her face into the pillow, feeling a little discomfited, and pointed towards the door that he walked out. Andrew stayed, staring at her sexy beautiful body and feeling tempted to touch. He parted her butts with his hands, exposing the inner walls of her extremely wet pussy. She threw her hand behind her, arresting his hands and then said, 'Just go away. Don't do this.'

He ignored her admonition, pushed her hand back onto the mattress and parted her butts again; this time, inserting his left forefinger into her pussy.

'Please stop it! I mean it, just stop! You can't do this.' She said sternly, ceasing his hands from moving any further.

Andrew could not believe she was so wet and yet suddenly pissed. For about five minutes, he remained seated on the bed without touching her and she had covered her butts, only still lying down. Her face was still stuck into the pillow.

He set his dick free from his tight boxer shorts and sat over her thighs. She could tell what he was about to do. She moved her hand behind her back to cease him from doing it but he pushed them away, opened her pussy and stuck his penis into it. Somehow, for some odd reason, she screamed and wrestled – albeit defenselessly – that he stopped but he wouldn't. He thrusted her from behind and fucked her roughly.

CHAPTER 3

In the morning, around 7:30am, Andrew woke up only to realize that Evelyn was gone. She woke up earlier, around 5am, and left just a few minutes afterwards. Andrew, seeing how messy and sperm-stained Tasha's bedspread was, hastily removed the bedcovers, soaked them into a bucket of water and replaced them with a fresher one.

He called Tasha's phone again but there was no answer. He took a shower and right afterwards, his phone rang. He guessed that was Tasha calling. He made his way lazily towards it and upon realizing it was Viola calling, he hastily answered.

She sounded very moody, sad and sober on the phone. He asked if everything was alright but she was reluctant to talk about it. They spoke for about five minutes and he cracked a couple of jokes to get her excited but all was in vain. Andrew opted to go see her and although she was skeptical but she agreed.

It was 9am when he set off and he reached her street a little over thirty minutes later. She came out of her home, directed him to the exact location of her house, and showed him in. He took a seat just beside her in a couch at the hall. The hall was quite big, about twice bigger than Tasha's and the house itself was some mini mansion of sorts.

Not long after he sat by her, she stood and told him she was gonna fetch them some breakfast. Andrew, after having sat down alone for over five minutes, walked his way into the kitchen where she was busy cooking breakfast.

He walked in stealthily, crept behind her back and startled her but she didn't see the funny side of it. Though she wasn't mad at him, she wouldn't let him stay with her in the kitchen. He insisted he wanted to help but she refused and walked him out, claiming she was almost done with it.

A few minutes afterwards, she set the dining table and they ate breakfast together. While they did, he realized she was persistently checking on her phone and calling someone's number but there was always no answer. After breakfast, Andrew picked up the bowls and headed towards the kitchen; much against her wishes. They washed the utensils and bowls together and afterwards, retreated to the hall.

Andrew sat in the double seated sofa, expecting her to sit by him but she took her seat in another.

'Hey, Viola' He said to her as she took her seat, 'why don't you come sit by me?'

'Oh… nothing. I'm just okay sitting here. Anyway thanks for passing by.'

'I can't believe you live alone in this big house. So you do all the chores by yourself?'

'Heck no! I live alone here but mostly, I spend the day at work and some nights at my fiancé's place. And about chores, I utilize the services of a cleaning agency. Their employees clean up my place.'

'Okay. you sounded really worried on the phone and even when I came, though you don't look very worried, you seem not to be very happy. Anything the problem?'

'Oh… Look, just forget about it.'

'Come on Viola, you know I care. I know you don't like to share your problems but you obviously needed someone to speak with. Have you been expecting a call?'

Tears began to drip down her eyes and her semi-bright facial expressions dropped totally. She wiped her tears but they wouldn't stop flowing. Andrew moved quickly towards her to cheer her up and he said, 'I'm so sorry, I shouldn't have said anything.'

She began sobbing. Andrew walked her to the bigger sofa, sat down with her, placed her head on his laps and consoled her. While on his lap, she took her phone again and tried calling once more. Andrew spied and saw it was Nick she had been trying to call.

'He's not picking your calls?' He asked, and she nodded.

'I don't know why and I'm only praying there's nothing wrong. I've been really worried since last night. He wasn't at his place when I got there and he's not answered my calls ever since.'

'Oh, that's bad. But does he do that often?'

'No, none that I can remember. I've been crying throughout the night. I have no friend to talk to. He's all I have and he's making me feel so incomplete.'

'I'm so sorry. I just hope he's not cheating on you.'

'Oh, no! Don't say that again!' She said sternly, 'He's not the kind of guy that cheats on girls.'

'Please forgive me, it won't happen again.' He said apologetically.

'It's alright. It's just that we've been granted a holiday leave from work and we were looking forward to spending the two weeks away from home. He has to come home so we discuss how to leave.

'Don't worry, he will surely come.'

Viola had a sleepy head because she had had almost no sleep during the night and so as they spoke, she fell asleep on his laps. He got himself up, slowly placing her head on the armrest of the sofa and laid the rest of her body into the sofa.

When Viola woke up, it was 12:30pm. Andrew was at the door collecting a food delivery he had ordered.

She went to wash her face, freshen her mouth and joined him. They ate and right after they were done, she told him it was about time he left because she had to go check up on Andrew again. They walked out of the house, she ignited her car's engine and drove off while he watched on. Andrew was glad that, at least, he was making a headway. He sat in his car and drove away.

CHAPTER 4

Viola arrived at Nick's home at 1:20pm. At long last, he called her but briefly – on phone – to inform her he was gonna come to her place soon but Viola didn't tell him she was already in his house.

About half an hour later, Nick drove into his compound only to find Violas' car parked among his cars. His heart beat suddenly; affrighted and confused because he had intended to wash down first and change before going to see her at her place.

He remained glued to the driving seat, unsure what to tell her and fearing what her reaction might be upon seeing him. Viola walked out of the house and made his way towards him. He loosened his seatbelt and got out of the car to meet her.

She had neither a smile nor a frown on her face; absolutely ambivalent towards him.

She hugged him without saying a word, took his suitcase from his hands and walked into the house with their arms wrapped around each other's waist. Not a single word dropped from anyone's lips until they got inside. They sat together in a sofa in the hall with her head placed on his chest and cuddled in his arms.

Moments later, she sat up and enquired from him in a soft sober tone, 'Where have you been Nick? I kept calling and you never answered.'

Nick couldn't look into her eyes. 'Um, uh…' He stammered.

'Don't even try lying to me Nick.' She said emphatically.

'No, I'm not trying to do that. Just don't know how to put it.'

'Well, just tell me why. Why couldn't you at least answer my call?'

'I met up with an old friend and we decided to spend some quality time together. We drove around town, went to his hotel, and then went out again to have a couple of beers. I got totally drunk and there was no way I could have made my way back home in that state. I slept at the hotel only to wake up this morning and find out I had lost my phone.'

She looked at him doubtfully and asked, 'Are you sure about this you're telling me?'

'Yes, I am.'

'And you can't even look into my eyes?'

'No, not that I can't look but you're just staring at me suspiciously and I don't like to see that face.'

'Hmm, so how did you manage to find your phone?'

'We went to check the various places we had visited and luckily for us, the security personnel at a golf park we had visited yesterday had custody of it.

They claimed someone had found it abandoned somewhere within the premises. Trust me, it's the truth.'

'Hmm, if you say so. What more have I to say? I was very worried, not that I'm not anymore but at least I have you now.'

'Viola, you know I love you. I'll never cheat on you.' He said assuredly, kissing her on the lips.

'I never said you cheated.'

They walked into his bedroom, she took off his suit and threw it unto the bed. He took off the rest of his clothing, laid her backwards on the bed and began to undress her. He slipped her panty off her legs, untucked her buttons, took off her brassier and began to kiss her breasts and bellybutton. Although she was very wet, she had her thighs tightly shut together. She stopped him in the process and asked him to go shower down before they would make out. He made his way reluctantly into the bathroom.

Just as he entered into the bathroom, she heard her phone beep – someone had sent her a text message. As she turned around to get it, she saw it lying right beside the ash colored suit she had pulled off Nick but something odd caught her attention. There was a reddish coloring somewhere on the suit. She checked the message and it was a text from Andrew that read: *"Hi Viola, I hope he's called you now and you've met up with him. I'm just checking on you to know if all is well. I wish you to be happy."*

She put the phone away after reading the message and picked the suit. She saw a faint pink coloring shaped like a human lip. Many suspicious thoughts began rushing into her mind. She couldn't get herself to believe Nick could have done what she was suspecting he had done.

Just to be sure, she searched his pockets for his phone that perhaps, she would see some pictures or messages attributable to it. She reached for his trousers and slipped her hands into the left pocket.

She pulled whatever was in there out and included in what came out was some pieces of paper and a torn condom wrapper. Her heart beat suddenly and tears began to drip down her eyes instantly like a waterfall. She got her hands onto his phone and tried unlocking it but it appeared he had changed his lock code.

She stood up from the bed, dressed quickly and began to make her way out. Just seconds after she left the room, he came out of the bathroom. He saw his trousers' pocket had been emptied completely onto the bed and the used condom wrapper was sticking out amongst the papers. He ran quickly after her and when he finally caught up with her, she was at the door of her car, about to open the door and enter in.

'Please Viola, let me explain; it's not what you think.' He said, kneeling and holding on to her hands.

'Just get off me! Let go! Fuckin let go!' She burst out angrily and tearfully, withdrawing her hands furiously and rudely from his grip.

She kicked him in the balls with her knees and he went tumbling to the ground in agony. She sat in her car and drove off straightaway.

CHAPTER 5

Tasha arrived home at 2pm that afternoon and met her brother sitting in the hall. He asked of where she had been the previous night but she brushed it off and walked towards her room.

He pursued her to confront her, suggesting she had spent the night whoring. Tasha was absolutely pissed that he had to imagine that. She believed he had no audacity to question her on where she had been since she was no more a child.

He tried to calm her down, saying that he didn't mean it the way he said it and that he only wanted her to find a responsible man whom she could settle with. She cooled down and told him the truth; that she was actually enjoying some sexual satisfaction throughout the night and in the early hours of the day too. However, she didn't let him in on the details. She asked him to walk out so she could get some sleep because she'd barely had any.

Tasha had been sleeping and Andrew had been feeling lonely. At 5pm, he called Viola to ask of her state since she hadn't replied his text message. He called twice but she didn't answer. Then he sent her a text message: *"Hey Viola, I'm not sure what's happening now but whatever it is, I just want you to know everything is gonna be okay. In the next ten minutes, I'll drive to your house if you don't call or reply this text. Perhaps, I could be of some help."*

Fifteen minutes passed but she neither called nor replied the text message. Since Tasha was still sleeping, Andrew set out of the house without her notice and drove towards Viola's house. Upon arrival, he rang the bell over and over and over again but there was no response. He sent her another text message: *"Hello Viola, I've been standing in front of your house for the past 15mins. Please open up if you're in or at least, message me to know whether or not you are in.'*

A minute later, he got a text message on his phone: *'Come to Galaxy Hotel, room A15.'*

He wondered what was up there, however, he sat in his car and set off to find the Hotel. Having driven for about 20minutes, he found the hotel and by 7pm, he was standing in front of room A15.

He knocked on the door and waited a short while but there was no response. He then knocked severally on the door for some few minutes but there was still no response. Then, he picked his phone and sent her a text that he was standing behind the door of room A15. Few seconds later, she unlocked the door but didn't open it.

He opened it slowly, peeped into the suite and saw her seated on a large bed. She looked very sad and even a kid could tell she'd been crying. He walked in and shut the door behind him. Then she said to him, 'Please lock it as well'.

He locked it and took a seat on the chair beside the bed, then he said, 'What's up Viola? What's with this hotel?'

'Look, just don't talk about it. I wanted to be alone but you wanted to come. Just hold it, keep mute, okay?' She said, quite rudely.

'Oh... It's alright. I'm sorry.'

'I just said shut up! Zip it!' She said sternly while throwing herself frustratingly onto the bed and covering her face with a pillow. Andrew watched her in absolute silence and could hear her sobbing but was quite confused about what to do. About ten minutes later, she sat up.

'Hey... Please forgive my attitude. I am... I'm just so broken right now.' She burst into another round of tears.

'Look, it's okay. Can I at least sit by you?' He said gently.

'Okay' she said tearfully.

He sat by her and cuddled her gently. She laid her head on his chest and wept even more uncontrollably. After a long period of silence, she opened up and told him what she'd just found out about her boyfriend. Andrew told her to cheer up, and that it was gonna be okay. After consulting her, he made an order for supper and they ate. Andrew managed to crack her enough jokes which bettered her mood.

At 9pm, she told him she had to go take a shower and that it was time for him to leave since it was getting late. He was a little bit reluctant to leave but since he had very little choice, he left. Ten minutes after he left her and was driving back home, he got a text message on his phone. He checked it out and it was a message from her; asking him if he could return to the hotel. Without a second thought, he turned around and drove towards the hotel.

He got there and she let him in. She had wrapped herself in a big white towel and she looked and smelled great. She turned around, right after opening him up, and walked towards her bed. He closed the door and sat by her on the bed.

'I shouldn't be in a towel but I actually didn't bring any other clothing along. I hope this doesn't cause a problem for us?'

'O… I'm cool with it.'

'You know what I mean right? I mean no problem. Keep your stick between your legs.'

'Come on, I'm not intending to do that.'

'Liars, all men are liars. I know it.'

'I don't think you should accuse us collectively. We are not the same, you know?'

'Whatever, I just can't trust anyone anymore. I called you over because I was thinking you would like to spend the night here.'

'Sure, certainly. With you, I'd really love to.'

'Alright, just make yourself comfortable but at least, go take your bath. I wouldn't want to smell the stench from your sweaty body all night.'

'Oh girl, now I think you're being very mean.' He said wryly, making his way towards the bathroom.

CHAPTER 6

Andrew slept by her side during the night but, unlike him, she wasn't able to sleep. Andrew woke up by 1am and found her still awake and sobbing.

Viola wiped her tears immediately she saw he was awake, nevertheless, he had already noticed she was weeping. In an attempt to console her, he stroked her gently on the arms and told her everything would be okay. She seemed to be enjoying it for a moment but after a while she lifted his arms off her suddenly, got out of the bed and walked into the bathroom. A minute later, she returned with her face washed and mouth rinsed. She sat on the bed and he sat up by her.

'Why did I invite you here in the first place? You are an absolute stranger.' She said rudely.

'Hey Viola, I've done you no harm. Just cool down okay, you're feeling hurt right now.'

'No! You're still an absolute stranger. The only difference is you've been stalking me.'

'Alright you win, but you could give yourself the chance to know me. I've been stalking you because I liked you immediately I saw you.'

'But you knew in the first instance that I have a boyfriend so what do you really want from me?'

'I did, but if I couldn't have you as my fiancé, I could still manage good friendship.'

'Yea, so that's it. You want me as your fiancé, just like that, right?'

'Yes, but not just like that. We could acquaint ourselves and then, who knows, you may begin to like me or perhaps, love me for a life partner.'

'And what about my fiancé? What happens to him?'

'Everything depends on you dear. Just give me as equal a chance as you've given him and let the heart take its course – Probably, you'd change your mind about him.'

'So that's it, right? You came to steal me from my boyfriend.'

'I wouldn't say *steal* per se but uh… I feel like I should fight for what I consider a treasurable asset.'

'I have the tickets for a holiday trip to Colorado Mountains and other tourist sites and the day is two days from now. I'm no longer going with him; I'll be going alone. Would you like to come with me?'

'Certainly, sure. Why not? I'd absolutely love it.'

'Alright, we leave in two days.'

'Alright, I'll prepare towards that.'

'You know what, why don't you just tell me you want to have sex with me?'

'Oh I do, but that's not my prime motive. I love you Viola.'

'Hey, just save it; those sweet-words don't work on me. I just shouldn't trust you. I'm off to bed.'

She lied on the bed, placed her head on the pillow and shut her eyes. He lied down too and kissed her on the forehead before resting his head on the pillow. She opened her eyes after some minutes and found him staring at her. Her eyes rolled away from his and made their way towards the lower part of his body. She could see – it was so clear – a big erection in his pants. She shut her eyes again, and began to contemplate on so many things. She imagined Nicky by her side at that time of the day and her eyes got a little teary again.

After some uncomfortable and anxious moments, still with her eyes shut, she asked him why he had an erection but he declined to answer. She opened her eyes and asked him once more but he only smiled back without saying a word.

Just when she was about asking the third time, he chanced on her lips with a kiss. She pushed him away, stopping him midway through the kiss, and turned her back against him. She was feeling a little ambivalent – sad about Nick's betrayal; furious at Andrew for kissing her; and glad that she was making a new friend who could turn out to be a nice person.

She turned around again and saw him lying on his back with his eyes shut but obviously not asleep and still harboring the strong erection in his pants. She also laid on her back – facing upwards – and loosened the towel, leaving her breasts, belly and pussy glaringly naked. She switched off the lights and shut her eyes.

Andrew, although with his eyes closed, noticed the lights had gone off. He opened his eyes and except for a dim beam of light penetrating through the sides of the window from the corridor, the room was very dark. He forced his sight through the darkness to catch a glimpse of her and when he did, he noticed her breasts and frontal parts of her body laid bare.

His erection hardened and he was beginning to go absolutely insane. He pulled his dick out of his boxer shorts and while still spying on her sweetly rounded sexy firm breasts, he began to pull on his penis slowly.

She opened her eyes but because of the darkness and his concentration on her nakedness, he didn't notice it. She spied on him from the left corner of her eyes and saw him spying on her nudity and fondling his dick. She was surprised and quiet impressed by what she saw – His dick was so big. He called her name and asked if she was asleep but she didn't respond. He called her softly, over and over again, for about four times but she still didn't answer. Thinking she was asleep, he slowly raised his right hands and sneaked them unto her breasts.

He caught her left nipple between his thumb and forefinger and fondled them gently. She began to feel a sexual sensation move through her body but she kept her feelings at bay, still pretending to be asleep.

He did it continually. After about five minutes, she was peaking in sexual longing. He moved his hand downwards, past her navel and towards her vagina but there was an obstruction – her thighs were tightly shut, leaving no access for him. He applied a little force to part them open but there was too much resistance in her thighs. He began to suspect she wasn't asleep at all.

He looked into her shut eyes and said, 'I know you're not sleeping. Why are you pretending?' but she still said nothing. He continued, 'if you don't say a word, I'm gonna kiss you.' Viola remained silent and unmoved. He planted a kiss on her lips but she didn't kiss back. He began to kiss her neck passionately and by then, Viola couldn't keep herself from moaning. After a few seconds, when she felt her defenses were being breached, he opened her eyes and pushed him off.

'What the fuck are you doing! Are you trying to rape me in my sleep?' She accused him.

'No Viola, I'm sorry but you know you weren't asleep.'

'Fuck you. How do you know whether or not I'm asleep?'

'You've got to be a little sincere Viola, you deliberately let your towel loose to entice me.'

She slapped him on the cheeks, covered herself in the towel and said to him, 'I have a fiancé. Respect that!' He pulled his boxer shorts back on, got up from the bed, took a pillow along with him and slept on the floor. She was extremely wet but just didn't want to have sex with someone who wasn't her lover and is a stranger. Andrew was so disappointed, embarrassed and pissed by her treatment.

CHAPTER 7

Around 7am the next morning, Andrew had left the hotel and reached his sister's house. He entered and made his way towards his room but before he would, he decided to check up on his sister.

He knocked on her door but the sound system in her room was so loud that she couldn't hear him. He opened the door and saw her on top of someone – busily fucking and screaming ecstatically. He shut the door immediately, went into his room and laid down.

An hour later, she called him to come eat breakfast. He was so pissed by what he had seen but he knew that his sister was no longer a girl and he had no right to question her life. He left the room ten minutes later to go have breakfast.

Upon reaching the hall, he saw his sister's fucker enter into his car and drive away while she waved him bye. He couldn't get to see the face of the person because he had a cap and sunglasses on but obviously, he was same height and weight as Nick – his prime suspect. Tasha walked in, feeling so excited and joined him at the table.

'Who was that guy?'

'Oh him… a friend.'

'Just a friend?'

'Yea, a very good friend.'

'You still don't have a fiancé?'

'No, but hopefully he would be my fiancé.'

'Are you sure that wasn't Viola's fiancé?'

'What! What? He's not the one. Why should you think so?'

'Well, cos I saw his picture among your books and the figure I saw getting into the car has his exact stature too.'

'No, no, he's not the one. I'll let you meet him but it will be a surprise. I won't disclose his identity to you.'

'He's the one you spent the night with the other time?'

'Yea, him.'

'He fucks you good, right?'

'Yea, certainly. But not as good as you used to fuck me.'

'Tasha! Fuck it! Damn! I told you to stop reminding me about this. We were young and silly, and it was absolutely out of place.'

'Well, if that's the case, why do you still have feelings for me? You're jealous when others fuck me, aren't you?'

'Screw you! I'm not jealous and I don't have feelings for you. I only feel for you as my biological sister and about your sex life, it's because I don't want people to just have their way with my sister and go their way, calling her a slut and cheap girl. When I hear such comments, I'm only hurt and not jealous.'

'It's been six years since we last did. Tell me you won't fuck me again if you had the chance.'

'You know what? You are so disgusting.'

'Oh please, don't even go there. Have you forgotten you broke my virginity? After watching dad's collection of porn movies, you were so horny. You made me watch porn too, seduced me, and deflowered me. You are rather disgusting.

How do you expect me to feel towards the guy who broke my virginity? Attraction of course. You are not just my brother but also the guy that gave me my first taste of sex and that attraction hasn't died away. Fuck you. You are disgusting!'

Andrew was so pissed. He got up, leaving his meal unfinished, and walked out on her but she pursued him to his room and sat by him on the bed.

'Where were you last night? You saw someone right?'

'Yes I did.' He rebutted rudely.

'And yet you're pissed I equally spent the night with someone. Are you insane?'

'Hey Tasha, I didn't fuck anybody last night.'

'Oh I see, but someone fucked you, isn't it?'

'No, I had no sex. Just get it into your head and get the fuck out of my room.'

'Really? Your room? You're in my house.'

'Well, I guess that's it. I've overstayed. I'm leaving right away.' He stood up to pack his belongings but she obstructed him, begging him not to leave. He insisted he was leaving and nothing she said could stop him.

By 10am, he was done bathing and had packed his things, ready to leave. He walked out of his room and got to the hall but he thought it would only be fair if he at least said goodbye to her.

He retreated to Tasha's room and turned the doorknob but it was locked. He knocked on her door severally but she didn't respond. He recalled that the last time such an argument occurred and he threatened to leave, she attempted suicide. He became anxiously scared and worried. He broke through the door and found her lying on the bed completely unclad, holding some pills in her hands and sobbing. He rushed towards her and snatched them out of her hands.

'Tasha, what are you trying to do? I'm sorry okay' He took her in his arms and cuddled her.

She said in a sober tone, 'I'm not trying to kill myself. These are the doctor's prescribed drugs. When I get nervous and extremely emotional, I take them. I've taken in two tablets already and that's the right dose.'

'I'm really sorry Tasha. You know I love you but, we can't be like we used to be. It was completely wrong.'

'I know, that's why I'm gonna be okay. My feelings for you and my lust for you has never changed, that's why sometimes I act like a slut but it's all to get you out of my head.'

'I'm sorry Tasha. Only if there was something I could do to help, I would.'

'It's alright, I took my pills and I'm gonna be just fine.'

'I'm not leaving anymore. I'll stay a little longer.'

'No, just leave right away. I'll feel worse if you don't. It's not easy seeing you around and yet not being able to touch you. Please go.'

'Okay, I will. But promise me you won't do anything silly. Please.'

'Right now, the only silly thing I want to do is kiss you. Just go away, I'll be fine.'

Andrew left, drove to Viola's house to pick the stuff she had asked him to retrieve while Tasha called Nick to come over.

He spent the day and the night with Tasha whiles Andrew spent the day with Viola. However, Viola booked the opposite room for him to spend the night because she didn't trust his sexual discipline.

CHAPTER 8

Viola and Andrew set off to the airport the next morning and they flew to go see the Colorado Mountains and some tourist sites.

Meanwhile, Nick had given up on calling her and searching for her; he was happily romancing with Tasha.

When they arrived at the airport, the 'Travel and Tours' team picked them up and drove them to the hotel. The various tourists were shown their suites but the day was far spent and the first tour was scheduled for the next day. Viola and Andrew had to share the same suite because that was the arrangement she had made when she thought she was gonna be there with her boyfriend. They ate supper and watched TV before going to bed around 10pm.

The weather was very cold because it was winter and though they put on the fireplace, it couldn't offset the cold temperature completely.

They laid on the bed for over fifteen minutes but Viola wasn't feeling comfortable and couldn't sleep. Andrew, although not asleep, was not talking either because he was feeling horny and was hoping to kill the urge and not fuel it. She got out of the bed, put on a winter coat, picked her mobile phone and walked out of the suite. He video-called Nick because she had missed him and was hoping they could sort things out.

Nick's phone rang. He was completely amazed and excited to see it was her. He stood up from beside Tasha who was lying beside him, walked to the hall and answered the call. He was very happy to see her and began apologizing to her right away. She didn't accept his apology but told him she had missed her and that she was still very hurt. She asked where he was because the background looked like no place in his house. He stammered, not knowing what to say but just as he was about to speak, Tasha had woken up from the bed and was walking towards him.

'Who's that in the background? Was she the one? Are you still with her?' Viola said almost tearfully.

He looked behind him and saw Tasha approaching him. She was still completely unclad. He turned around to get Tasha's image out of the cameras, but when he checked the screen, Viola had dropped the call. He called back immediately but she didn't answer. He tried again but she had switched her cellphone off.

'Was that your fiancé?' Tasha asked.

'Yes.' He replied coldly.

'I'm ruining your relationship right?' She said sadly.

'It's not you. It's me who is messed up. Even at college, when I was dating you, I was still indecisive, unstable and unfaithful. I thought that was because you were slutty but I realized the problem is with me.'

'I'm really sorry about this. It's her you love. Forget about me and be with her.' She said bluntly and returned to the bedroom.

Viola was so hurt and mad at him. She returned to the suite, threw her phone into the sofa, took off the snow jacket and began to strip off her clothing as she joined Andrew in the bedroom. Andrew starred at her. He noticed she was very furious but couldn't tell why she was. She went completely unclad and joined him in the bed but turned his back against him. His dick sprang up instantly with a jet speed but he declined to touch her.

'Viola, is everything okay? You look pissed.' He said soberly.

'I don't look pissed, I look naked. Just fuck me. Isn't that what you want?' She said tearfully but rudely.

'No, I love you and would want to make love to you; not fuck you.'

With her back still turned against him, she said, 'Take off your shorts.'

'What?' He asked surprisedly.

'I said take off your fucking shorts!'

'No, not like this. Not while you're pissed.'

She turned around, sat on him and began to pull off his shorts and boxer shorts. When he tried stopping her, she slapped him on the cheek, pushed him back onto the bed and pulled them off. She grabbed his dick, but though scared of the humongous size, she put it into her mouth and began to suck aggressively on it. She gave him the best blowjob of his life. When she was done, he picked her up, laid her on her back, spread her thighs open and drew his dick towards her pussy. He tried penetrating but she wasn't the least wet in her pussy. He halted.

'Viola, you're not the least wet. It's gonna hurt you.'

'Fuck hurt, I'm already hurt.'

'You are doing this because you're hurt and not because you love me?'

'You know what? I'm hurt and I'm also scared of your monster dick. Just get me wet and fuck me. No more words.'

Andrew looked her in the eyes but she looked away. While groping her breasts, he stuck his mouth into her pussy and sucked incessantly on her clits like a hungry baby sucking on her mama's breastmilk. Though still very furious, it was too sweet to contain. She moaned uncontrollably. In some few minutes, she was completely wet and began to experience a shaky orgasm. She screamed loudly and withdrew her squirting pussy away from his lips with a bittersweet look on her face.

'Fuck you. What did you just do to me?' She said with a big smile on her face. He held her legs open and inserted the tip of his dick into her pussy.

'Fuck! It's so big.'

'And it's so wet. Should I withdraw?'

'No, please, just enter me.' She said in a sober subdued tone.

He pushed his dick further into her and she just couldn't stop herself from screaming.

'Does it hurt?'

'No, it's just twice as big as Nick's and it's so sweet. Just fuck me.'

He pulled out and thrusted even deeper and deeper – she melted in ecstasy. After about fifteen minutes of relentless penetration and screaming, she forced his dick out. Her pussy squirted uncontrollably and her body twitched and twerked involuntarily. He slipped his dick into her pussy again and pounded her over and over, until midnight.

At 2am, while they were asleep, gunshots were heard in the hotel. They woke up and were extremely terrified. They could hear screams and incessant gun shots being fired. They ran into the bathroom and locked it up.

The gunshots drew closer and closer and closer. Suddenly, they heard a big thump on the door to their suite. The door fell and they could hear footsteps in the room. Viola began to fidget and cry but he held her mouth firm. The criminals tore the room apart and banged on the bath door. Since they refused to open it up, they shot at the knob and locks. A leg in a black trouser stepped in and Viola's heartbeat surged exponentially, just like Andrew's. Andrew covered her eyes with his hands and shut his as well. Instantly, they heard multiple gunshots fired within the suite and they screamed at a deafening volume.

They thought they were dead but they heard a voice say, 'Fly one reporting, room 17 clear. I repeat, room 17 clear. Medics needed.' Andrew opened his eyes and saw a man in a mask lying in a pool of blood.

He was completely terrified and when Viola looked, she was even more terrified. The rescue team picked them up from the floor of the bathroom and drove them off to a secure ground while the medics attended to the shot civilians and criminals.

The next day, the news was reported and it was a nationwide story. The attack had been carried out by a militant group which caused the death of twenty-five persons and eleven severe casualties. Andrew and Viola had received the worst scare of their lives. They lost complete interest in the tour and they flew back the same day, after they had been cleared by the FBI.

CHAPTER 9

Despite Andrew's frantic efforts to win her love, Viola sorted things out with her fiancé a month later and they came back together. Andrew returned to New York, his permanent place of abode.

Three months had passed since the ordeal. However, Viola had been harboring a major worry. She was three months pregnant and wasn't sure which of the two was responsible.

She had kept her sexual encounter with Andrew a secret from Nick. On one Saturday, per her doctor's recommendation, she took an HIV/AIDS test and the results came out positive. She was extremely shocked by the news and she wondered how and when that could have been. She thought it through and suspected her fiancé must have infected her. She became extremely mad at herself for allowing him back into her life.

She drove to Nick's house, entered and sat at the hall. He came in, excited to see her but she was obviously so angry and very sad. He sat by her but she got out of the seat simultaneously and broke the news to him, accusing him of infecting her. The news sent shivers down his spine but he disagreed vehemently, arguing that probably she rather had infected him.

They drove off to the hospital and he got tested positive too. He boiled with rage. When they sat in the car, he finally told her the truth that the lady he had cheated on with was Tasha – his ex-girlfriend and sister of Andrew – and they had sex in a bathhouse that very night at the soiree.

She was extremely mad at Nick and he also was so mad at Tasha. They drove to Tasha's house.

When they got there, Tasha was having lunch with her friend Evelyn at the dining. She wondered what could be the purpose of their visit but seeing their faces from a distance, as they walked towards the door, it was so obvious they were upset. They entered and immediately, Viola punched her in the face, accusing her of being a cheap slot.

Nick sat down, declining to stop her from assaulting Tasha. Tasha, though much a stronger figure than Viola, adopted a defensive approach because she knew Viola was carrying a baby. Evelyn rushed from the dining to her friend's defense, keeping Viola at bay. When Viola realized she couldn't lay her hands on Tasha anymore, she broke the news and accused her of infecting her fiancé with HIV. Tasha denied and argued vehemently that she wasn't infected.

Tasha argued that if the test results were true, then Nick could have infected them both since he wasn't the least a faithful fiancé. Nick rose his arm to hit her in the face but exercised some restraint, turning away furiously and making his way back into the seat.

Tasha also accused Viola, claiming there was no evidence that she had never cheated on him. Tasha accused her of possibly infecting Nick who had in turn infected her as well, only if that was the case. Tasha was so furious that they had to accuse her of something she hadn't done. She walked into her bedroom, returned with a pistol and pointed it at them. Viola and Nick rose to their feet and pleaded that she put the gun down but she wouldn't listen. She commanded them to sit in the sofa and when Evelyn tried calming her down, she got furious at her, pointed the gun at her and asked her to join them in the sofa.

'Now tell me, when was the last time you cheated and with who?' She queried Viola with the gun pointed at her.

She shivered, stammered, and said, 'W-w-w... With your brother. With Andrew, when we went to Colorado three months ago.'

'What the fuck? Shit!' She boiled with rage. 'You fuck my ex and my brother?' Nick was absolutely stunned and dumbfounded but couldn't say a word.'

'No, please, it's not what you think. Nick broke my heart and while I was so pissed and emotionally unstable, I wanted a payback.' Viola said tearfully.

'You are telling me bullshit! You mean you've infected my brother too?'

'No, I swear I was never infected. Until then, I had no other sex partner other than Nick and even with Andrew, it happened just once. It never happened again.'

Tasha went absolutely crazy and shot Nick right in the head. They all screamed and were extremely terrified. She pointed the gun back at Viola who had already eased on herself out of terror. She cocked the gun, ready to shoot her but Evelyn stood in the way to cover her.

'Please stop. She's innocent, shoot me instead.' Evelyn pleaded.

'Get out of the way Evelyn!' Tasha said sternly.

'No Tasha, shoot me instead. It's my fault. I knew I was HIV positive but the night I came searching for you and you weren't around, I slept with your bro without a condom. I infected him.'

'No! No! It can't be. Tell me it's a lie.'

Evelyn insisted it was the truth. Tasha called Andrew to find out and he admitted that they had sex that night. She dropped the call. She was so furious at Evelyn and felt betrayed.

Evelyn sat on the floor and wept bitterly. Viola was still sitting in the couch with Nick's corpse and was fearing for her life. After about two minutes, Tasha told Evelyn she still loved her as a sister and wouldn't be able to shoot her even though she really wants to. Tasha told them to remind her brother that she always loved him. She pointed the gun to her own head and shot herself dead.

They screamed at the peak of their voices and were terrified by the sight they were beholding – Tasha's head burst open and her right eye bulged out of its socket. Police sirens could be heard approaching from a near distance. Viola ran out of the house to throw up and seconds after getting out, she heard another gunshot from within the house. She ran back and saw Evelyn had shot herself too. Evelyn did so because she felt very guilty for the deaths and wasn't ready to live the rest of her life with that burden on her shoulders.

Andrew arrived later in the day after hearing the news. He was broken upon hearing the details of the incident from Viola's lips. Six months later, after their burials, Viola delivered a baby boy. The good news – he wasn't infected with the virus. Though the paternity test proved he was Andrew's she named her after Nick. Three years later, having finally outgrown the ordeal, she agreed to be marry Andrew.

I like to write great romance stories that take you on an emotional journey whether tears, laughter (or both) or just steamy hot fun (or all of them).

Please... leave a review, let me know if you had enjoyed read this great story?

THANK YOU ☺

www.ingramcontent.com/pod-product-compliance
Lightning Source LLC
Chambersburg PA
CBHW071350130626
46556CB00005B/2122